CW01023182

Usborne Farmyard Tales

Poppy and Sam's Fairy Stories for Bedtime

After a busy day on Apple Tree Farm, Poppy and Sam love to have stories read to them before bedtime. They snuggle up together and lose themselves in magical tales of fairies and adventure. This book is full of the stories they like best, so you can enjoy them too.

Usborne Farmyard Tales

Poppy and Sam's Fairy Stories for Bedtime

Based on stories by Philip Hawthorn

Illustrated by Stephen Cartwright

Adapted by Kate Nolan

Additional illustrations by Simon Taylor-Kielty

Designed by Reuben Barrance

 There is a little yellow duck to find on every double page.

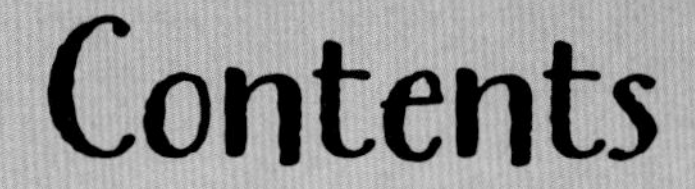

Contents

Polly and the Pixies

One day, Polly was hurrying home from market. Her mother was unwell, and they needed money to pay the doctor, so she had been to sell a gold ring. It was a long journey. As she walked quickly through a small village, she passed some people on the green.

"You're in a big rush for such a little girl!" a woman said to her. The others nodded, agreeing. "You must be tired. Why don't you stop for a rest?"

Exhausted, Polly did as they asked.

The villagers fussed and chattered around her. One man brought her glasses of water, and another offered to hold her bag as she drank.

"What kind people," Polly thought as she set off again, feeling much better. But later on, she looked inside her bag, and her heart sank.

Her money was gone. The bag was full of stones.

"I've been robbed!" wailed Polly, bursting into tears. "The villagers must have taken all my money while I was having a drink! And I didn't even notice!"

A fairy who was flying past stopped to comfort her.

"Please don't cry," said the fairy. "I'll call the pixies. I'm sure there's something we can do."

She whistled, and suddenly they were surrounded by pixies with long beards and pointed ears.

"Polly here needs your help," the fairy told them. The pixies crowded around and listened carefully as Polly told them what had happened.

When she had finished, the pixie chief said, "Me thinks it's time for a pixie fair."

"A pixie fair! A pixie fair!" chorused the others.

"What's a pixie fair?" asked Polly.

The chief pixie replied, "Well now, we sets up our stalls, and we sells pixie things like this." He picked up a pine cone from the ground, and swirled it around very fast. When he opened his hand, the pine cone had turned into pure gold.

"Here," he said, throwing it to her. "This is for you."

"A pixie gift! A tricksy gift!" sang the others, and disappeared.

In a twinkling, they were back, bringing with them the most beautiful stalls. Then they used their magic to turn pieces of tree bark into chunks of gold, spiders' webs into the finest silver, and dewdrops into sparkling diamonds. In no time at all, the stalls were piled with precious things.

When the fair was ready, the pixies skipped off to find the villagers.

"Come to the fair! Come to the fair!" they chanted. Then, dancing around the startled people, they sang:

"Flobbity-wee and flibbity-woo,
A pixie fair we have for you,
With gold and silver, diamonds too,
Come to the pixie fair!"

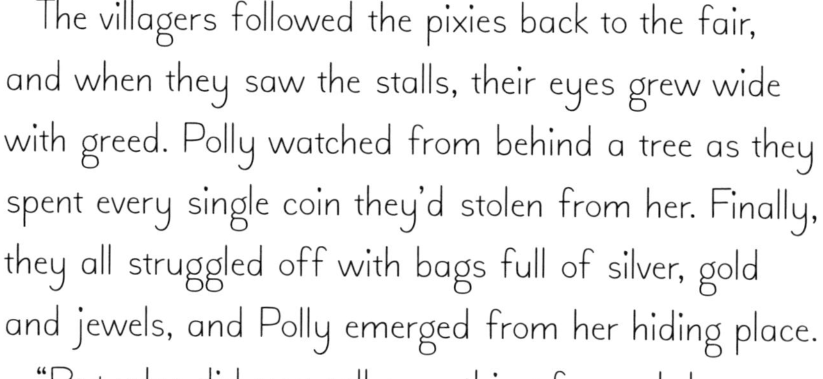

The villagers followed the pixies back to the fair, and when they saw the stalls, their eyes grew wide with greed. Polly watched from behind a tree as they spent every single coin they'd stolen from her. Finally, they all struggled off with bags full of silver, gold and jewels, and Polly emerged from her hiding place.

"But why did you sell everything for such low prices, after how they treated me?" she protested.

At this, all the pixies laughed loudly.

"Watch this!" said the chief. He waved one of the treasures, and it changed back into a normal leaf.

"All those precious things will turn into ordinary things again," said the fairy. "And we've got your money back."

The pixies gave the bag full of coins to Polly. "Farewell!" they sang, and vanished.

"Now," said the fairy, "I think you'd better be going, too." There was a bright flash, and Polly found herself at home. Smiling, she showed her mother the money and the golden pine cone.

The villagers were horrified when they realized they'd spent all that money on bags full of leaves and bark. Polly's mother soon got better, and Polly never forgot her adventure with the kindly pixies.

Angel

There was once a fairy girl named Angel, who wasn't at all like an angel. In fact, she loved to play mean tricks on the other fairies. One day, Angel was hiding behind a bush, hoping to scare her friend Flutterby. She heard footsteps, so she leapt out, shouting "BOO!" But it wasn't Flutterby. It was a human boy. Angel disappeared instantly, but she knew she'd been seen.

"Ugh! A human!" she said to herself. "I expect he thinks he's really clever to have seen me, but I'll show him." She followed him to find out where he lived, then went back to her mother. She had a plan...

"Mother," she said, innocently. "If anyone hurt me, would you be angry? Would you punish them?"

"Yes, I would," replied her mother. "Why?"

"Oh, um... no reason," said Angel, and she flew off to the little boy's house, where he was getting ready for bed.

"Oh, hello," he said, recognizing Angel at once.

"Hello. I'm Angel," said the fairy, smiling a little too sweetly. "What's your name?" But the boy could tell that Angel had a trick in mind, and he had a plan.

"My name is Me Myself," he said, although of course it wasn't.

"Let's play chase," said Angel, flitting away from him. "Catch me!" She was much quicker than him, though, and he couldn't even get close.

But after a few minutes, the naughty fairy fell to the floor, holding her knee. "Ooohh!" she wailed. "You hurt me, you clumsy human boy."

"I didn't touch you," he said (which was true).

"Yes you did! Yes you did! Yes you DID!" said Angel. "I'm going to tell. MO-THER!"

In the flicker of a candle, her mother appeared. "What's the matter, Angel?"

"Someone's hurt my kneeee," Angel whined. "Will you punish them?"

"Yes. Who did it?" came the reply.

Angel smiled spitefully at the human boy.

"The person who hurt my knee was Me Myself," she shouted.

"I see," said her mother. "Well, if it was you yourself, then I will have to punish you yourself."

She waved her magic wand, and Angel found herself back in her own bedroom. Her mother didn't let her go out for a week. Angel learned her lesson after that, and never played a trick again.

The Hairy Boggart

Farmer George was on his way home one evening when he found a mischievous, hairy boggart looking greedily at his field.

"I wants a chit-chat," it said. "I wants you to grow lovely-jubbly grub for tummy-rumbly boggart."

George couldn't afford to let the boggart take his crops, so he knew that he'd have to find a way to get rid of it. He thought quickly and said, "We could go halves on the next harvest." Too lazy to argue, the boggart agreed.

"Do you want tops or bottoms?" asked George.

"Umm, topsies," replied the boggart. "See you at harvest." And off it went.

The clever farmer planted a field of potatoes. So when the boggart returned at harvest time, it got the useless leafy tops, and the farmer kept all the lovely potatoes that had grown underground.

"Next time, I wants the bottomsies," growled the hairy boggart. And off it went.

The farmer now planted wheat. So this time, the boggart just got the dry stalks from the bottom, while George got all the golden grains of wheat that had grown at the tops of the stalks.

"You skillywig!" said the boggart angrily. "Next year, you grows corn. We cuts it together and keeps what we cuts." The boggart was stronger than George, so it would be able to harvest most of the crop.

But George soon came up with another cunning plan. The day before the corn harvest, he painted some iron rods golden-yellow to match his crop, and stuck them in one end of the field.

The boggart arrived the next day, carrying a scythe. "Right, ready steady?" it said. "Let's go."

"You start over there," said the farmer, pointing to the end of the field where the iron rods were hidden among the stalks of corn.

The iron stalks were very difficult to cut, and they blunted the scythe. The hairy boggart was soon tired and cross. Finally, its scythe snapped, and so did its temper. It ran off, roaring loudly. Farmer George smiled to himself and carried on cutting. He was never bothered by boggarts again.

The Endless Story

One evening, Orlando was walking along the beach when he saw a mermaid sitting on a rock, combing her hair. Hearing his footsteps, she jumped with surprise.

"Mermaids should never be seen by humans. You have seen me, so I must grant you a wish," she said. "Take this comb and meet me here tomorrow evening. But come alone, and don't tell anyone." Then she slipped silently into the sea and was gone.

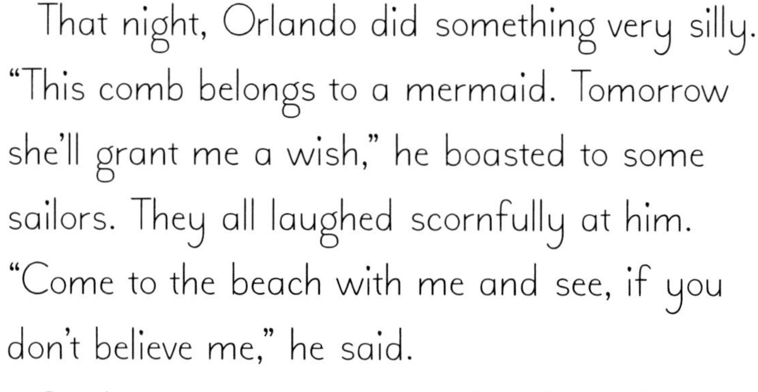

That night, Orlando did something very silly. "This comb belongs to a mermaid. Tomorrow she'll grant me a wish," he boasted to some sailors. They all laughed scornfully at him. "Come to the beach with me and see, if you don't believe me," he said.

So the next evening, the sailors hid behind a boat on the shore, and watched as Orlando went to meet the mermaid. As soon as she rose from the sea, they rushed forward and grabbed her.

Suddenly, they heard a loud roar. There was a flash, and Orlando and the sailors found themselves in the palace of Neptune, king of the sea fairies.

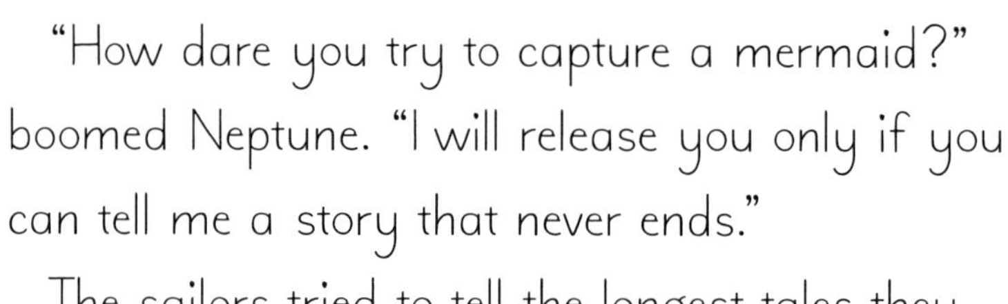

"How dare you try to capture a mermaid?" boomed Neptune. "I will release you only if you can tell me a story that never ends."

The sailors tried to tell the longest tales they could, but no matter how hard they tried to spin out their stories, eventually they all dried up.

Finally, it was Orlando's turn. So he began.

"A man decided to polish the beach. He picked up the first grain of sand and polished it, then he picked up the second grain of sand and polished that, then he picked up the third grain..."

Orlando's story went on and on and on and on. When he got to the two hundred and sixty-fifth grain, Neptune shouted,

"Stop! Stop! That's enough. I'll let you off this time, but you've been warned." With a look of relief, he waved his trident, and Orlando and the sailors were transported back to the beach.

Orlando never got his wish, but he didn't mind. He was very glad to be home.

Sniffer

There were two things that Sniffer always had: a purple silk handkerchief and a cold. That was why he was called Sniffer, because his cold made him sniff all the time.

One day, Sniffer was walking to the market. He didn't have much money, but he needed some food for supper. Suddenly, he came upon a leprechaun sitting on the ground, mending a shoe. Sniffer remembered his grandmother's advice. "If you ever see a leprechaun, catch him and don't let go," she had said. "Ask where his pot of gold is buried, and he'll have to tell you."

So Sniffer reached out and grabbed the leprechaun's arm. "Gotcha!" he called.

He was surprised when the leprechaun just laughed.

"Ah! That's caught me well and good, so it has," he giggled. "You've got the better of me."

"Yes," replied Sniffer, a little uneasily. "Now I want your pot of gold."

"Well, if you let go of me, I'll lead you to it." But Sniffer remembered his grandmother's warning.

"I know what you're up to, you little pickle," he said, holding on even more tightly. "Now it's gold time!"

Unable to wriggle free, the leprechaun started out across the fields. Eventually, they came to a huge field of beautiful poppies.

"The gold is under this poppy," said the leprechaun, pointing to one. "Dig down deep and you'll find it."

"I just need to go home and get a shovel," said Sniffer. "How will I know which is the right flower when I get back?"

"I'll wait here and tell you," the leprechaun replied, his eyes growing brighter.

"I'm not falling for that," said Sniffer. Then a thought came to him. He reached into his pocket and pulled out the purple handkerchief. "Tie this to the poppy." The leprechaun did as he was told.

"Promise me that you won't take it off."

"I promise," said the leprechaun. Sniffer let go of the leprechaun and ran home.

When he got back to the field, he saw that the leprechaun hadn't removed the handkerchief... but he'd tied identical handkerchiefs to all the other poppies.

It would take Sniffer years to find the right one.

"Oh, cabbage," said Sniffer. But at least he now had plenty of silk handkerchiefs. By selling some of them, he earned enough money to buy some food for supper, and that night, he cooked a delicious meal for his wife. He never did find that pot of gold, though.

The Brave Shepherd

Charlie the shepherd was out for a walk one day when he saw a tiny silver flute lying on the ground. He picked it up, put it to his lips and blew. There came a pure, sweet note, and a fairy appeared.

"You've found my flute! Oh, thank you!" she said. "Let me give you something as a reward."

She reached into her pocket and gave Charlie a small, round, white thing. "This is a magimint," she told him. "When you eat it, you will know exactly the right words to say." And off she flew, playing her flute.

Charlie put the magimint into his pocket and walked on. A little later, he passed a beautiful palace. Some grand-looking people were talking excitedly outside, and Charlie saw a poster on the door.

HIS ROYAL MAJESTY KING ARCHIBALD
SEEKS A HUSBAND FOR HIS DAUGHTER,
HER ROYAL HIGHNESS PRINCESS PETRONELLA.
A TEST WILL BE SET TODAY.
ALL WELCOME.

"You're just in time for the test, sir," said a guard, ushering Charlie inside.

"Oh well, I might as well give it a try," thought Charlie. "I bet I'm as strong and fast as any of this bunch." Then he saw some small writing at the bottom.

ALL WHO FAIL WILL BE ARRESTED.

"Arrested!" thought Charlie in dismay. "I need to get out of here, quick!"

But before he could think of how to escape, some big doors opened, and in came the king and princess. They sat down on their golden thrones.

The king looked nervous. The princess looked sulky.

"My lords," said the king. "Here is your test. I have decided that the princess shall marry whoever can say the bravest words. Is that all right, my dear?" He looked at Princess Petronella.

"Don't care," she said, without the slightest interest.

"And, of course, the rest of you will be thrown into the dungeons," continued the king. "Who's first?"

The candidates began to call out to the princess.

Each was trying to outdo the one before.

"I could battle a dragon," cried one.

"I could defeat two fierce dragons," yelled another.

"I could slay a hundred huge, hungry dragons!" shouted a third.

And so it went on, until there was only one person left. The king glanced at his yawning daughter. She didn't look impressed.

"You, boy," said the king, pointing at Charlie. "You're last."

Charlie walked up to the throne. His face was frozen in panic and his knees were like jelly.

Suddenly, he remembered the magimint the fairy had given him. He put it into his mouth. All at once, it felt as if his tongue had a mind of its own.

"Your Majesty. Did you hear about the dragon who was an actor? She became very flame-ous."

There was a shocked silence.

"How dare you!" bellowed the king. "Guards...!" But suddenly he heard a sound that made him stop. The princess was laughing! The king had never seen her laugh before.

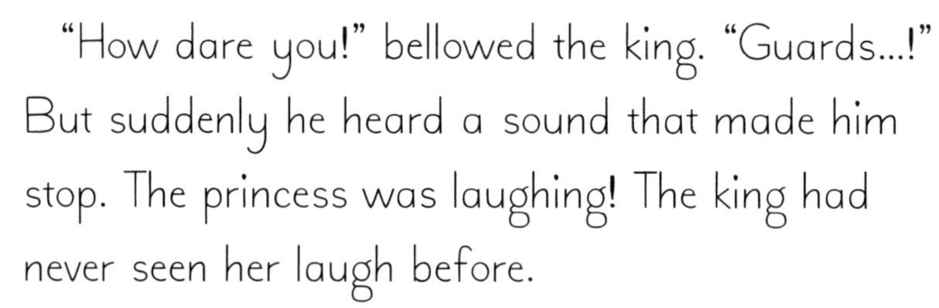

"The rest of you just tried to show off," she said, giggling. "At last, someone has made me happy."

"Come to think of it, telling a joke was incredibly brave... you win, my boy," the king said.

So, a few months later, Charlie moved to the palace. He and Princess Petronella were married, and they lived a long and happy life together.

Mr. Bibbleberry's Bath

Mr. Bibbleberry was rude and selfish. His heart was as hard as cement, but his company, Bibbleberry Bubbles, made the best bubble bath in the land. It smelled sensational.

The river that ran behind the factory didn't smell very nice, however. It had a strange green tinge; the fish were often ill, and so were the river fairies. In the end, two of them went to ask Fairy King Oberon for help.

"It's not fair," said Pondweed. "We try to look after the river and everything that lives in, on or by it."

"The situation is very, very bad," said Ripple.

"I know," said Oberon. "I think we should go and have a look around Mr. Bibbleberry's factory."

They made themselves invisible, flew into the factory, and came to a noisy room filled with pipes, tanks and tubes. There was a wonderful smell of lemon.

"This is the room where they make the bubble bath," said Oberon. Then he led them through a door marked 'Waste Room'. The smell was terrible.

"Yukkity ugh!" said the sprites.

"You see, whatever you make, there's always waste," said Oberon. "It's like with cooking. You can make the tastiest food, but there's always something, such as carrot tops, onion skins or egg shells, to get rid of. Let's see what Mr. Bibbleberry does with the waste from his factory, shall we?"

They found a pipe which ran from the room and followed it outside. Thick gunk was pouring from the end, straight into the river.

"Stinky-poo!" said Pondweed.

The three fairies decided to have a word with the factory owner, but when they got to his house, he just shouted at them.

"Buzz off! I'm about to have my bath. I want to try out my new lemon bubbles."

The fairies left, but not before Oberon had waved a magic spell over the new bottle.

Early the next morning, the fairies flew to the market square, and what they saw there made them gasp. Mr. Bibbleberry was sitting in a bath of cement. Oberon's spell had changed the bubble bath to cement powder, which had set in the water. It had also moved the bathtub to the middle of the town.

"Get me out of here!" fumed Mr. Bibbleberry.

"I'll help you if you clean up the river," said Oberon.

"Never!" said the arrogant man. "I'm not going to be ordered around by a bunch of fairies."

"Suit yourself," said Oberon as they flew away. "You'll only be free when you've found a way to say you're sorry."

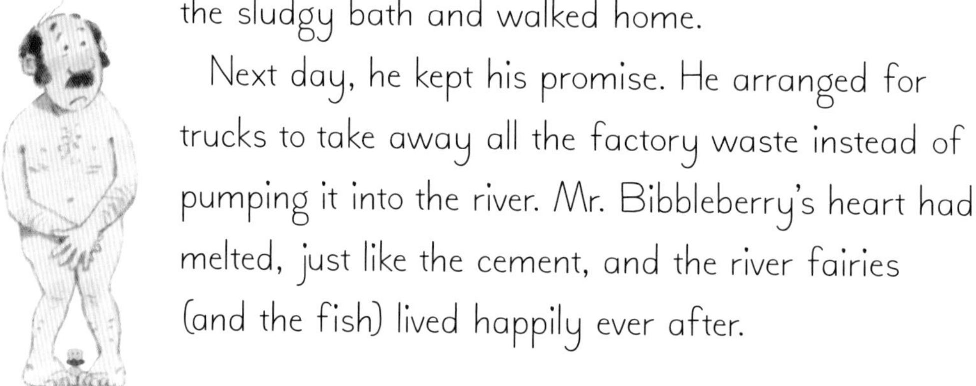

Soon, Mr. Bibbleberry was hungry and cold. Even worse, people were laughing at him.

"All right," he yelled as night fell. "I give in! You win! I know how awful the river is! I will change things, I promise!" But no one came to help him.

In the end, he started to cry. And as the tears fell onto the cement, they melted it. He climbed out of the sludgy bath and walked home.

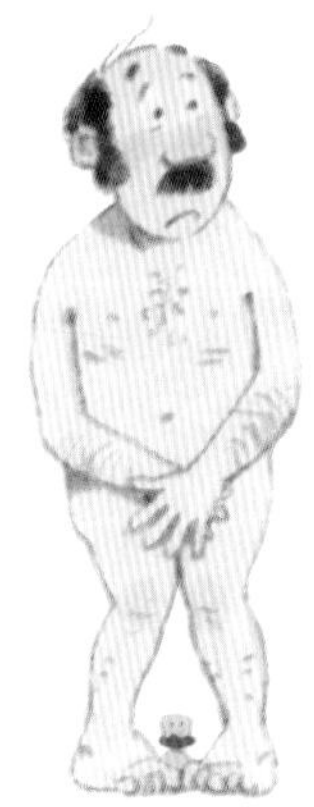

Next day, he kept his promise. He arranged for trucks to take away all the factory waste instead of pumping it into the river. Mr. Bibbleberry's heart had melted, just like the cement, and the river fairies (and the fish) lived happily ever after.

The Tooth Fairy

Alice liked collecting things. Unfortunately, they were things that made her parents say, "Oh, please! Really, Alice!" She had a scab from when she'd cut her knee, a dead spider she'd found in the bathroom, and lots more. She kept everything in matchboxes, which her father called her horror boxes.

When a tooth fell out, however, there was no way she'd keep it: teeth were for the tooth fairy.

Alice had a loose tooth when Aunt Megan arrived to celebrate her birthday with Alice's family. Aunt Megan was very loud, gave the most disgusting kisses, and hated the horror boxes even more than Alice's parents did.

"Come and give your auntie a kiss," said Aunt Megan. Alice saw the big, red lips coming towards her, and then... Slurpy-Slobber! Perfume-Smelly! Sticky-Wet kiss. Eeyuurrgh!

The kiss was so hard that not one, but both of Alice's front teeth came out. She spat the teeth into her hand and held them out, saying, "Aunt Megan, look!"

"Oh my goodness!" Aunt Megan wailed, turning pale. "How re-volt-ing!" She didn't even say sorry. Alice turned and stomped crossly up to her room.

Suddenly, an idea came to her. She put one tooth under her pillow as usual. But the other tooth went into a matchbox, which she wrapped up in birthday paper.

"Happy birthday, Aunt Megan," she chuckled to herself as she got into bed.

In the middle of the night, Alice woke up. To her great surprise, there was a fairy on her pillow, carrying Alice's tooth and a sack.

"You're the tooth fairy," said Alice. "Where do you take all the teeth?"

"Come with me and I'll show you," said the fairy. She took Alice's hand, and off they flew.

First, they visited the bedrooms of sleeping children. The fairy left a coin under each pillow and put the teeth in her sack. Then they flew to the North Pole, to collect a baby polar bear's tooth from under its pillow of snow. And finally, they went to a smoky-hot mountain for a huge dragon's tooth, which lay under a pillow of hot coals.

After that, they flew for ages, until the fairy started to dive towards a ring of mushrooms in a field. Nearer and nearer, faster and faster they got, until Alice was so scared she closed her eyes.

"Hold on tight!" called the fairy.

Scrunch! Whizz! Fizz! Whooooosh!

Alice opened her eyes. The moon seemed enormous, and the stars twinkled brightly. The trees and the river glowed in the moonlight.

"Welcome to Fairyland," said the tooth fairy.

Soon, they came to a brightly lit house where lots of other fairies were working. All the teeth they had collected were being washed and put into a pot. Then the fairies gathered around, pointing their fingers at the pot and singing a fairy song. The air shimmered with magic, and when the pot was uncovered, it was full of dazzling, shiny pearls.

"We're the only fairies with this magic," said the tooth fairy, proudly. "In this pot were all sorts of teeth, and each one has made a perfect pearl!"

Alice was amazed, but it was time to go home. As they flew back, tired from her busy night, she dropped off to sleep.

She woke in her own bed. Had she dreamed it all?

"Time to get up, Alice!" came a yell from downstairs. "It's Aunt Megan's birthday."

Alice dashed down the stairs with her present, but as Aunt Megan was opening it, Alice suddenly remembered the tooth inside. She turned red and tried to think of an excuse to leave, but it was too late.

Aunt Megan opened the matchbox.

"Alice!" she said, her eyes widening. "How absolutely... wonderful. Thank you, darling!"

Alice couldn't believe it. The tooth had vanished, and in its place was a pair of beautiful pearl earrings. Aunt Megan was happy, and Alice wasn't in trouble – thanks to the tooth fairy.

The Silly-Willies

"It's strange," said King Dominic one day to his old friend, Whizz the magician. "The people in my kingdom have been very silly lately. Yet whenever anyone says they're silly, they get very upset. They're a right bunch of silly-billies."

"It sounds more like the Silly-Willies," said Whizz. "They're naughty fairies who whisper silly ideas into people's ears while they're asleep. It puts them under a Silly-Willy spell. Don't worry. I'll look into it."

Next day, as Whizz was walking into town, he met two very frightened-looking men.

"What's the matter?" asked Whizz.

"We're worried about that apple," said one, pointing up into a tree.

"Why?" asked Whizz.

"Well, what if there was a storm?" said the man anxiously. "With snow and wind? The apple would blow off the tree... and roll down the hill... and as it rolled it would make a huge snowball... and what if a small girl was standing in its way... and it squashed her?" The men both burst into tears.

"It would be so terrible," they sobbed together.

"Yes," said Whizz. "But what if it didn't snow? After all, it is the middle of summer."

"What would you know?" they said, and walked off.

Whizz carried on walking and reached the town. Suddenly, from inside a house, he heard:

Thump-thump-thump-thump... Crash! Ow!

Whizz knocked and went inside. In the bedroom upstairs was a man who had hung his jeans on a chest of drawers. He was trying to put them on by running up and jumping into them, but he kept crashing into the drawers and hurting his knees.

"Why don't you step into them and pull them up with your hands instead?" said Whizz.

"What would you know?" said the man, rudely.

As Whizz left the house, he heard:

Thump-thump-thump-thump... Crash! Ow!

Later that evening, Whizz came upon some people standing around the town pond, looking concerned.

"The moon's fallen into the pond," a woman told him.

"That's only its reflection," said Whizz.

"What would you know, smarty-pants?" she said.

"I'll show you," he replied. He took a stick and stirred up the surface of the water, shattering the reflection into a million rippling fragments.

"He's broken the moon!" shouted a man. "Get him!"

They chased Whizz all the way back to the castle, where he told King Dominic all about the mayhem that the Silly-Willies had caused in the village.

"What can we do?" said the king.

"Well," began Whizz. "The Silly-Willies get into people's bedrooms through keyholes. If everyone blocks them up, they'll move on somewhere else. As they aren't in the castle, you needn't bother."

The king told everyone in the town to block their keyholes, and next day, everyone was back to normal. So Whizz got ready to leave.

"I can't thank you enough," said the king. "But where are the Silly-Willies now?"

"Who knows?" replied the magician. "They could be anywhere. Thanks for having me. Goodbye."

But as Whizz rode off on his horse, King Dominic began to gaze in horror at the moon's reflection.

"Whizz!" he shouted with all his might. "Whizz! Come back! The moon has fallen into the moat!"

The Magician's Assistant

Alex was a magician's assistant, although he hadn't learned any magic yet. He worked for Madge, a good magician who used her spells to help people. In her house was an amazing spell room, full of bottles and books, funny-shaped equipment... and lots of dust.

One morning, Madge and Alex were starting work.

"Let me get the spell book for you," said Alex.

"Alex, you know you're not to touch my spell book," said Madge. "Magic is a serious business. Good magic and bad magic are often not that far apart."

Alex sulked. "When am I going to do some magic?" he grumbled. Ignoring him, Madge opened the book and got to work.

"Let's see. I'll need some powdered chestnut, three tears of laughter and some caterpillar skin." Alex collected them and gave them to Madge.

"Thank you," she said, mixing them together. "All I need now is some fluff from the pouch of a kangaroo." Alex went off to find the jar.

"It's empty," he called from the cupboard.

"Oh, bother," said Madge. "I'll have to go and get some. I won't be long. Make a start on the cleaning up, please, but don't touch my spell. Toodle pip." And off she went. Alex looked at the mess and sighed.

Just then, Catsby, Madge's cat, gave a loud meow and jumped onto the spell book. This gave Alex an idea. Leafing through the book's pages, he came to a Tidying Up Spell.

It looked quite easy really. He gathered the ingredients and mixed them together. Then came the magic words.

"Ibblibum bottium, wibbly wobblium..." he chanted. But Madge's handwriting was so hard to read that he started to make mistakes. "Um... capsicum... is that... sillius billium?"

He was just about to give up when there was a huge thunderclap. From a cloud of green smoke came a tall, green man with large, hairy ears. Alex froze.

"O most gracious master," said the creature, bowing. "I am your loyal servant, Hairylugs. Your wish is my command."

"Great!" said Alex. "Would you tidy up for me, please?"

"Of course, master," said Hairylugs. Jars and bottles rattled onto their shelves as he whirled around the room, putting things away.

Then things started to go a bit wrong. The creature began to tidy Madge's bench. Alex asked him to stop, but Hairylugs just ignored him and carried on. Madge's new spell was swept into the waste bin. Catsby was put away in a cupboard.

"What now, O master?" said Hairylugs.

"Um, nothing. You can go, thanks," replied Alex.

"What NEXT?" boomed Hairylugs.

Alex began to feel a bit scared. Instead of calling a helpful fairy, he had called a mischievous goblin, who was now yelling, "I want an ORDER!"

Alex said the first job that came into his head. "Water the plants."

"Of course, master," sneered Hairylugs. He started to water the plants with a huge bucket, which he kept on filling and emptying over the pots with a great Sploosh!

"Stop! Stop!" cried Alex, as the water rose around his ankles, but Hairylugs kept going. Sploosh!

Suddenly, the door burst open and Splo-WOOSH! Madge was knocked over by a tidal wave.

She took one look at the room, lifted her wand and challenged Hairylugs to a battle of magic. Alex crouched behind a chair, wide-eyed, as spells exploded all around.

Then Madge came across the waste bin containing her spell. She took the kangaroo fluff from her pocket and mixed it in.

When she yelled the spell at Hairylugs, he screamed and disappeared in a cloud of green smoke.

"Phew!" said Madge. "I'm glad I was working on a spell to get rid of goblins." Alex thought he was going to get the biggest scolding of his life, but Madge just smiled as she closed the spell book and put it away on a high shelf. "You see, a few wrong words can be all that separates good magic from bad magic."

Alex thought it might be a while before Madge let him anywhere near the book again, but he didn't mind at all. As he let Catsby out of the cupboard, he decided that, from now on, he'd stick to doing his own tidying up.

The Fairy at the Well

Once there was a man who lived with his two sons. The elder, Oscar, was exactly like his father: good-looking, grumpy and greedy. The younger son, Kevin, was very kind. But the father treated Oscar like a prince and made Kevin do all the hard and horrible jobs around the house.

One day, when Kevin was at the well fetching water, an old woman approached him.

"May I have a drink, please?" she asked.

"Of course," said Kevin, pouring some water into a jug for her.

The woman was really a fairy in disguise. She said, "Thank you. From now on, with every word you say, a flower or precious stone will fall from your mouth."

Back at home, Kevin's father barked, "You're late."

"I'm sorry, Dad," said Kevin. Two tulips and a ruby fell onto the kitchen floor. His father's eyes burned with greed. Then he made Kevin tell him what had happened, which made more jewels and flowers fall. When Kevin had finished, his father sent him to clean out the pigsty, and called Oscar.

"There's an old woman down at the well," he said. "Give her some water and she'll give you something amazing."

"Do it yourself," said Oscar rudely.

"Go! NOW!" shouted his father.

Crossly, Oscar stamped all the way to the well. He had just arrived when a young woman came up to him.

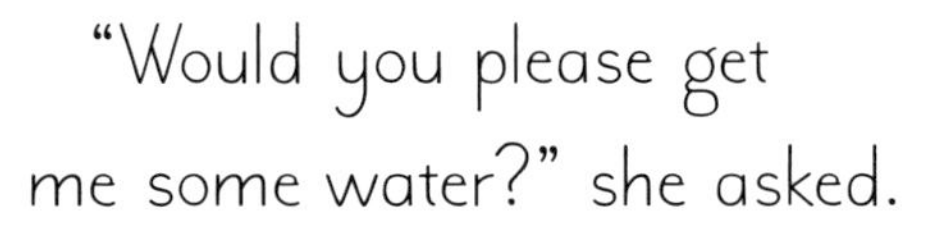

"Would you please get me some water?" she asked.

"Get it yourself," Oscar sneered, still sulking.

Unfortunately for Oscar, the girl was really the same fairy as before.

"How unkind! Every word you speak shall turn into something horrible," she said. Then, she disappeared, leaving Oscar alone.

When Oscar got home, his father said, "Well?"

"I didn't see her," puffed Oscar. Three rotten eggs and a dead beetle fell from his mouth.

"Ugh!" yelled the father. "This is Kevin's fault."

Oscar moaned so much that the house was soon filled with nasty things. So after a while, Kevin decided that it was time to leave home. He lived happily for many years, using his riches to help others, and it was all thanks to the fairy's gift.

The Disobedient Dog

"Here, Alfie!" yelled Mr. Truffle at his disobedient dog. But Alfie just sat down happily in the middle of the park. Mr. Truffle sighed and walked on.

When he reached the park gate, he turned and shouted, "Alfie, come HERE!" Alfie sniffed the air, then lay down on the grass.

"Well, blow me down!" said Mr. Truffle, turning red. "Why can't my dog do what he's told?" He walked out of the gate in the direction of his house. Eventually, Alfie got up and wandered after him.

Mr. Truffle reached his house, and was about to close the door when Alfie walked in and started to scratch. Hairs, twigs and grass went everywhere.

"Well, blow me down!" grumbled Mr. Truffle. "What a disobedient dog!"

Next day, Mr. Truffle walked Alfie in the woods. He threw a stick, but instead of chasing it, Alfie trotted off in the opposite direction.

Suddenly, there was a flash. A small dog appeared, with a golden collar and tiny wings.

"Hello," it said. "I'm your furry dogmother. Name a wish and it shall be done."

"Well, blow me down!" said Mr. Truffle. "I wish Alfie would obey me."

The fairy dog wagged its tail in a shower of shimmering stars. "He will now obey every single word you say." Then it was gone.

Mr. Truffle rubbed his eyes. "Well, blow me down!" he said again. "It must have been a dream. Come on, Alfie!"

The next thing he knew, Alfie was by his side, wagging his tail. Mr. Truffle stopped, amazed.

"Are you feeling all right, Alfie?" he asked. Alfie stared at him, panting eagerly.

Mr. Truffle stared back. "Sit," he said at last. Alfie obeyed. "Roll over." Again, Alfie obeyed. Mr. Truffle picked up a stick and threw it. "Alfie, fetch!" Alfie set off like a streak of lightning, grabbed the stick with his mouth and tore back to Mr. Truffle. He dropped the stick at his feet.

Mr. Truffle couldn't believe it. He scratched his head and said, "Well, blow me down!"

But unfortunately, the magic was still working, so Alfie obeyed. He took a deep breath - and blew Mr. Truffle down!

Fairy Nuff

Fairy Nuff was a small and slightly scruffy beginner fairy. Her magic didn't always go exactly to plan, but it never seemed to matter too much.

One day, there was great excitement in the woodland because Fairy Queen Mab was coming to visit. The fairies had decided to put on an amazing show for her, with lots of different acts.

"We'll take turns dancing, singing, or doing whatever we feel Queen Mab would like," said Larkspur, a senior fairy. "But we must keep this visit a secret. If the hobgoblins hear about it, they're bound to spoil it."

The next day, Fairy Nuff started planning her act. She wanted to do something splendid, something surprising and spectacular... but what? Thinking hard, she wandered along under the trees.

Then she stopped and yelled,

"A magic firework display! Brilliant!"

"What are you doing?" came a voice.

She looked up and saw a crow on a branch.

"It's a secret for Queen Mab," she said.

The crow's eyes lit up. "Really? When's she coming then?"

"I'm not allowed to tell you that it's this evening," said Fairy Nuff.

Unfortunately, the crow wasn't really a crow at all. It was Gobby, the chief hobgoblin, in disguise. He hurried away, chuckling to himself, and soon thought up a horrible plan to ruin the royal visit.

That evening, Queen Mab arrived in a beautiful water lily coach pulled by dragonflies, and the celebrations began. Willow played her harp, Larkspur sang a song and Appleblossom danced on a large mushroom. Some other fairies put on a play. Everyone cheered and clapped.

Queen Mab was delighted, and the fairies were all having such a lovely time that no one noticed the hobgoblins. They were giggling as they planted hundreds of smelly-spells in the flowerbed. When set off by magic, these spells would erupt, spraying out jets of stinky, sticky, gooey slime.

At the celebrations, Fairy Nuff was the last to perform, but she was so excited that she tripped over. As she hit the ground, her firework spell shot into the flowerbed and set everything else off too. Flowers, spells and hobgoblins whooshed into the air in great clouds of green, blue and gold.

The smelly-spells went so high that the fairies couldn't smell them. They just saw huge fountains of flowers and beautiful, magical sparks. But the hobgoblins got covered in stinky slime. Grumbling, they slouched off.

"Thank you, Fairy Nuff," beamed Queen Mab, as the fairies' celebrations continued. "That was the best flowerwork display I've ever seen!"

Fairy Nuff and the Monster

One morning, some villagers awoke to a terrible disaster. A girl named Julia had disappeared. Only Molly, Julia's little sister, knew what had happened, but no one would listen to her, so she went to the wood outside the village and started to cry.

Suddenly, her sobs were interrupted by a wild screeching. She looked behind a bush and saw a small, rather scruffy fairy with a magic wand, yelling madly.

“Whoops-a-buttercup,” said the fairy. “Just trying out some spells. Sorry, um, I'm Fairy Nuff.”

“I'm Molly,” said Molly, and burst into tears again.

“What's wrong?” asked kind-hearted Fairy Nuff. She listened as Molly told her all about her sister's disappearance.

“She was grabbed by a huge monster with the most enormous eyes I've ever seen.”

“It sounds like Big-Eyes!” exclaimed Fairy Nuff. “I've heard all about him. He's horrible. Rescuing Julia might be tricky.”

“Will you help me?” said Molly.

“Of course I will,” said Fairy Nuff. She didn't tell Molly that she was only a beginner fairy. She just grabbed Molly's hand, waved her wand bravely and said, “Let's go!”

Fairy Nuff's spell took them to a cave in a snowy mountain. Unfortunately, they appeared right in front of Big-Eyes, who spotted them straight away.

"Aha! Even more supper for me!" he boomed. Molly and Fairy Nuff could see Julia locked up in a cage nearby. She looked terrified.

"Stop! Don't eat us!" cried Fairy Nuff frantically. "We've got something for you."

Big-Eyes paused. Even hungry monsters like presents. "What is it?" he said.

"Um... it's a... ummm..." said Fairy Nuff. Then an idea struck her. Maybe some music would send him off to sleep. "It's a concert," she said.

She waved her wand, and immediately in Molly's hands there appeared some bagpipes. Molly began to play them, and, with the help of the magic, managed quite a good tune.

"Lovely!" said the monster. "It reminds me of my grandpa. When I was a mini-monster, we used to dance before I went to bed." Then he got up and jigged around the floor. He was enjoying himself so much that his huge eyes were open wider than ever. He didn't seem sleepy at all.

Finally, he said, “Now I’ll have my supper.”

“Is that what you used to do after you danced with your grandpa?” asked Fairy Nuff.

“Don’t be silly,” said Big-Eyes. "It was bedtime, he used to tell me a story. A lovely story about Baby Big-Eyes.”

“Well, that’s your second surprise,” said the quick-thinking fairy, and she immediately launched into a story. “Once upon a time, in a far-away land, lived a baby monster...”

When she’d finished the story, there was loud snoring. Fairy Nuff had worked an amazing trick. The monster was very tired after all that dancing and excitement. So he’d closed his huge eyes for a nap.

Quickly, Molly helped Julia out of the cage, and Fairy Nuff managed to magic them all back to the village. The delighted villagers held a huge party that evening, and Fairy Nuff was the special guest. She stood on the table and made a speech.

"You don't need to worry any more about Big-Eyes," she said. "He'll be so embarrassed that he won't dare show up around here ever again."

The Vinegar Bottle Woman

There was once a woman called Mrs. Funnybones, who lived in a vinegar bottle. One day, a kind fairy named Skip was fluttering past the bottle when she heard Mrs. Funnybones talking to herself.

"Dear-oh-dearie me," she moaned. "Imagine me only living in a bottle. I ought to live in a pretty little cottage."

Skip listened to these complaints, and then she said,

"Just shout 'Wazoomer!', blink your eyes,
Tomorrow morning, big surprise."

Mrs. Funnybones did as she was told, and the next morning she awoke in the prettiest little cottage you could imagine, with a thatched roof and roses around the front door.

Mrs. Funnybones loved her cottage at first, but the next time Skip flew by, Mrs. Funnybones was complaining again.

"Dear-oh-dearie me. Imagine me only living in a little cottage. I ought to live in a big house on a busy street."

Skip listened patiently, then said,

"Just shout 'Wazoomer!', blink your eyes,
Tomorrow morning, big surprise."

Mrs. Funnybones did as she was told, and in the morning she found herself in a bigger bed, in a bigger house with a shiny brass knocker on the front door.

Mrs. Funnybones loved her house at first. However, on Skip's next visit, Mrs. Funnybones started complaining again. "Dear-oh-dearie me. Imagine me only living in a house. I ought to live in a mansion." Again, Skip listened, then said,

"Just shout 'Wazoomer!', blink your eyes,
Tomorrow morning, big surprise."

Sure enough, Mrs. Funnybones awoke the next morning in a beautiful four-poster bed, in a huge mansion with a lake in the garden.

Skip was sure that this time Mrs. Funnybones would be happy, but no! Not long after, she began to complain again.

"Dear-oh-dearie me. Imagine me only living in a mansion. I ought to be a queen, and live in a palace."

Skip couldn't believe her ears. But she was very kind, so she said:

"Just shout 'Wazoomer!', blink your eyes,
Tomorrow morning, big surprise."

Mrs. Funnybones became Queen Mrs. Funnybones. She travelled to other countries, met important visitors, and lived in a beautiful palace with lots of servants.

But a while later, as she flitted past the palace, Skip heard something that almost made her wings fall off.

"Dear-oh-dearie me. Imagine me only being queen of one country. I ought to be the Ruler of the World."

Skip sighed. She didn't think Mrs. Funnybones would ever be content. So, for the very last time, she said:

"Just shout 'Wazoomer!', blink your eyes,
Tomorrow morning, big surprise."

Next morning, Mrs. Funnybones had the biggest surprise of all. She wasn't in a palace. She wasn't in a mansion, or a big house. She wasn't even in a pretty little cottage. She was back in her vinegar bottle, and there she stayed.

The Nose Tree

Wendy was running through the woods. She was so poor and so hungry that she had just stolen a doughnut from the market, although she knew it was wrong. As she sat down beneath a tree to eat it, she disturbed a fairy, who quickly fluttered out of reach.

"That was close!" she said. "If you'd captured me, I would have had to grant you a wish." At this, Wendy wept. A wish would have solved all her problems.

"Oh, please don't cry," said the fairy. "You can have this instead."

She waved her hand, and Wendy's doughnut became a silver bracelet.

"It glows when magic's around," said the fairy, and she vanished.

A few days later, Wendy was walking through a large city when a procession came along. A guard was calling, “Make way for Prince Handsome! All must look upon his radiant beauty.” The prince was handsome, and he knew it, because he kept glancing into a golden mirror as the people obediently watched him pass.

Just then, Wendy noticed a bun that had fallen on the floor. She was hungry, so she bent to pick it up.

“Stop! That person is not looking at me,” called the prince in a stern voice, pointing at Wendy. “Guards! Arrest her at once!”

Wendy was taken back to the palace and left alone in a room. Her bracelet began to glow, and looking inside a cupboard, Wendy found the fairy who'd given it to her. She was locked up in a glass box with a huge padlock.

"The prince caught me," she said sadly. "He wants a wish."

"What will he wish for?" asked Wendy.

It was the prince himself who answered her. "To rule the world!" He was standing behind her, his eyes bright with the thought of such power.

Wendy noticed that he'd left the door open behind him. Thinking quickly, she ducked past him and ran as fast as her legs could carry her out of the palace.

Back in the forest, Wendy's bracelet started glowing again. Looking up, she saw a strange-looking tree, heavy with huge, shiny apples. She ate one, and her nose grew to an enormous length.

"Thanks, bracelet," she said with a huff. It was still glowing, and she saw that next to the apple tree was a pear tree. She ate a pear, and her nose grew back to the normal size again. Then, she had a brilliant idea.

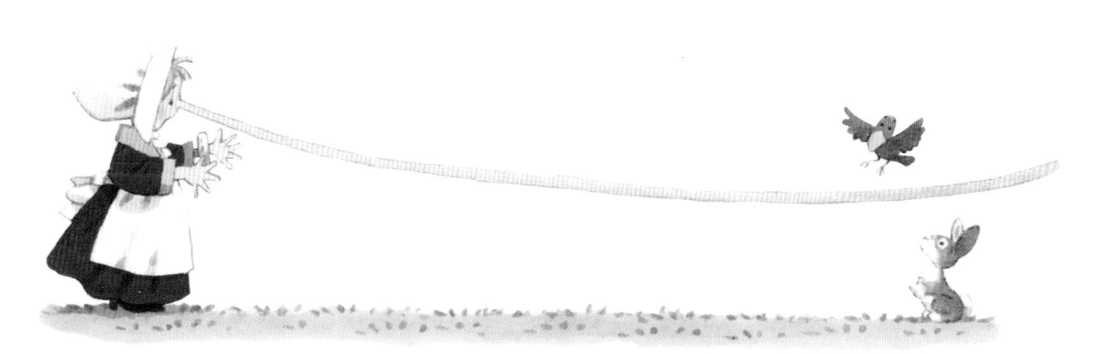

Disguised as an old woman, Wendy left a basket of the magic apples outside the palace. When the prince saw them, he said, "What splendiferous apples! Bring them into the palace for my lunch."

Later, Wendy returned, still in disguise, with a bag of pears. When she got to the palace, she saw that her plan had worked. The prince was sitting forlornly on the palace steps, and his nose seemed to stretch for miles.

"My magnificent looks! Ruined!" he wailed as Wendy approached. "What can I do?"

"I am a doctor, and I can help," said Wendy.

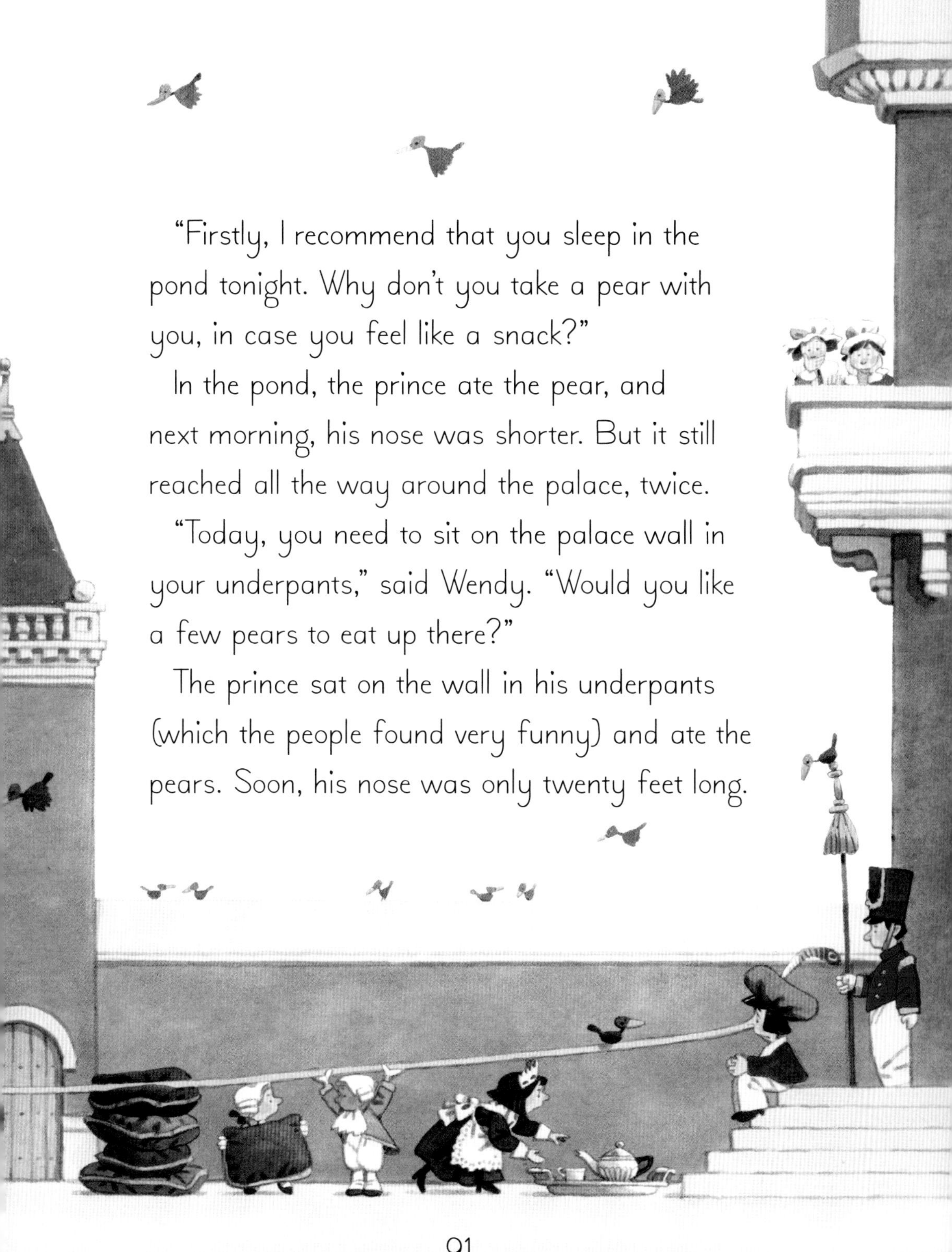

"Firstly, I recommend that you sleep in the pond tonight. Why don't you take a pear with you, in case you feel like a snack?"

In the pond, the prince ate the pear, and next morning, his nose was shorter. But it still reached all the way around the palace, twice.

"Today, you need to sit on the palace wall in your underpants," said Wendy. "Would you like a few pears to eat up there?"

The prince sat on the wall in his underpants (which the people found very funny) and ate the pears. Soon, his nose was only twenty feet long.

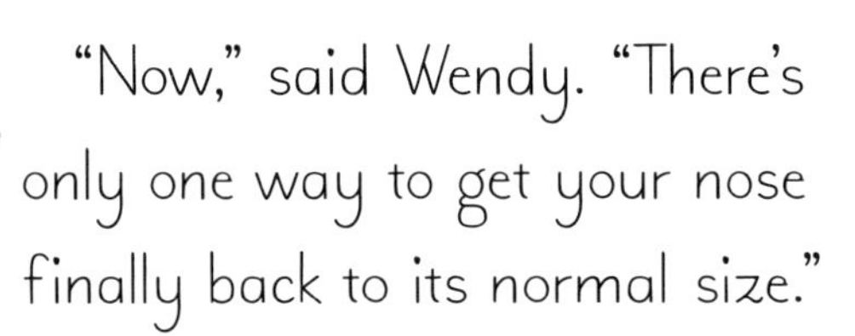

"Now," said Wendy. "There's only one way to get your nose finally back to its normal size."

"How?" he said. "I'll do anything, anything at all."

"Release the fairy," said Wendy. So he did.

"I shall make your nose the right size," the fairy said. "But if you ever say how good-looking you are again, it will grow back." To the prince's great relief, she magicked his nose back to normal. Then she looked at Wendy. "Thank you very much for all your help." She smiled at her, and disappeared.

"I can't thank you enough," the prince said to Wendy. "Please accept this as a reward for your excellent advice." He gave her a big bag full of golden coins, and Wendy left the city, overjoyed. She knew that she would never go hungry again.

Crafty Herbert

When strange things happened in the village of Bomford, it was always the fault of Crafty Herbert. He was a shape-shifting fairy, which meant he could become anything he wanted in the blink of an eye.

In a cottage on the edge of the village lived a cheerful, kind woman whose name was Nancy. She grew pretty flowers in her garden, and this pleased the fairies.

But Crafty Herbert wasn't pleased. He got fed up with them all constantly chattering about how lovely Nancy was. So he decided to play some tricks on her.

One day, Nancy went to milk her cow, who was called Moo. She didn't know that Crafty Herbert had hidden her cow and turned himself into one exactly the same.

Normally, it took Nancy half an hour to milk Moo. Today, it took three hours. The cow just walked away every time she sat down on her stool.

Finally, she managed to do some milking - but as soon as she'd finished, Crafty Herbert kicked the bucket so that the milk went all over her.

Nancy was speechless with rage. She turned and walked briskly back to her house, followed by the muffled sound of mooey laughter.

Tricks like this went on for weeks, until Nancy couldn't stand it any more. She went to see the Wise Woman, who lived in a cave near the village. The Wise Woman could tell exactly what was going on, and she told Nancy all about Crafty Herbert.

"But he only plays tricks when he knows it's annoying someone," she said. "He hates it when people laugh at him. Why don't you try that?"

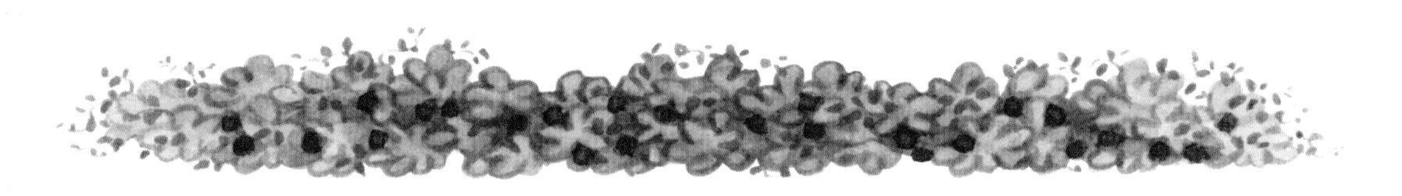

The next day, Nancy was trying to work in her strawberry patch. Unfortunately, Crafty Herbert had transformed himself into a puff of wind and kept blowing things around, making it very difficult for her to do anything. She wanted to scream with rage, but she remembered what the Wise Woman had said and roared with laughter instead.

"Another wonderful trick!" she chuckled, looking not at all annoyed. This made Crafty Herbert rather cross. He puffed harder and harder, making the leaves in the garden rustle madly. Nancy's dress billowed in the wind, but she just kept on laughing.

At last, Crafty Herbert had had enough. With one final, enormous puff, he flew off in a sulk. Nancy watched him go, then smiled to herself as she carried on with her gardening.

Nancy lived quietly and happily in her little cottage for the rest of her days. The fairies often fluttered around her lovely garden, but Crafty Herbert never played a trick on her again.

The stars are twinkling above Apple Tree Farm, and Poppy and Sam are drifting off to sleep. Night-night everyone...

Cover illustration by Simon Taylor-Kielty
Edited by Sam Taplin
Additional designs by Kate Rimmer
Digital manipulation: Keith Furnival

First published in 2020 by Usborne Publishing Ltd.,
Usborne House, 83-85 Saffron Hill, London EC1N 8RT, England.
usborne.com